Leave it to PET!

The Misadventures of a recycled Super Robot

Leave It to PET Vol. 1

STORY & ART BY Kenji Sonishi

Translation/Katherine Schilling
Touch-up Art & Lettering/John Hunt
Cover & Book Design/Frances O. Liddell
Editor/Traci N. Todd

Editor in Chief, Books/Alvin Lu
Editor in Chief, Magazines/Marc Weidenbaum
VP, Publishing Licensing/Rika Inouye
VP, Sales & Product Marketing/Gonzalo Ferreyra
VP, Creative/ Linda Espinosa
Publisher/Hyoe Narita

MAKASETE PET KUN Vol. 1
© Kenji Sonishi 2004
All rights reserved. Original Japanese edition published by POPLAR Publishing Co., Ltd., Tokyo. English translation rights directly arranged with POPLAR Publishing Co., Ltd., Tokyo. The stories, characters and incidents mentioned in this publication are entirely fictional.

Printed in the U.S.A.

Published by VIZ Media, LLC
P.O. Box 77010
San Francisco, CA 94107

10 9 8 7 6 5 4 3 2 1
First printing, April 2009

vizkids

www.vizkids.com

store.viz.com

VIZ MEDIA

Contents:

PET's Haiku p.4

CHAPTER 1 **PET Is Born!** p.5
CHAPTER 2 **PET Repays the Favor** p.13
CHAPTER 3 **PET Transforms!** p.21
CHAPTER 4 **PET Goes Round and Round** p.29

CHAPTER 5 **Multilingual PET** p.37
CHAPTER 6 **PET, the One-Bottle Rescue Team** p.45
CHAPTER 7 **PET to the Rescue!** p.53
CHAPTER 8 **PET Goes to the Dogs** p.61

CHAPTER 9 **PET Cleans Up!** p.69
CHAPTER 10 **Meet Plaz!** p.77
CHAPTER 11 **Meet Alu!** p.85
CHAPTER 12 **PET's Piggy Bank** p.93

CHAPTER 13 **Meet P-2!** p.101
CHAPTER 14 **PET vs. P-2** p.109
CHAPTER 15 **It's Alive!** p.117
CHAPTER 16 **PET, the Recycling Ninja** p.125

CHAPTER 17 **This Is PET's Home Base** p.133
CHAPTER 18 **PET's Secret Gadgets** p.141
CHAPTER 19 **A PET for Every Occasion** p.149
CHAPTER 20 **Meet Tiny Tin!** p.157

CHAPTER 21 **Charge It Up, PET!** p.165
CHAPTER 22 **Meet the Can Crew!** p.173

PET's Special Bonus Tracks! p.181

PET's Haiku*

RECYCLING IS GOOD!
PROTECT THE EARTH AND MAYBE
PET WILL THANK YOU TOO!

*A haiku is a type of Japanese poem
that is three lines long. The first line
has five syllables, the second has
seven, and the third has five again.

CHAPTER 1
PET Is Born!

6

7

8

9

10

12

CHAPTER 2
PET Repays the Favor

I AM A SUPER ROBOT SENT FROM THE RECYCLING PLANT TO REPAY NOBORU FOR RECYCLING ME.

Recycling Plant

MY NAME IS PET.

NOBORU!

ZOOM

PET!

WHENEVER HE'S IN TROUBLE, I'LL BE THERE.

...PET!

THANK YOU...

RECYCLE...

...WHOMP!

I'LL USE ALL MY POWER AND STRENGTH TO PAY HIM BACK IN FULL!

ZWOOSH

14

17

IT IS!

HEY, IT'S GOOD!

GULP GULP GULP

LOOKS OK...

WHAT THE--? YOU JUST BOUGHT THIS!

SAYS HERE, "YOU'LL LOVE THE TASTE!"

OOH, FANCY.

IT'S MADE FROM 100% SUN-RIPENED VALENCIA ORANGES FROM CALIFORNIA.

MAGIC WORDS?

NEXT TIME YOU NEED SOMETHING, JUST SAY THE MAGIC WORDS.

OH, YES! ONE MORE THING...

THAT'S IT?!

NOW I'LL TAKE MY LEAVE...

PLUS, IT'S HARD!

ONE TINY SLIP-UP AND IT WON'T WORK!

I'LL SOUND LIKE AN IDIOT!

PA-PI-PU-PE! PI-PU-PE-PO! PO-PU-PE-PA PET!

CHAPTER 3
PET Transforms!

22

HUH?

HEY, COULD YOU GIVE ME A HAND WITH SOMETHING?

MY BATTERIES ARE ABOUT TO RUN OUT!

SUPER ROBOTS HAVE NEEDS, TOO!

UH, YOU'RE SUP-POSED TO HELP *ME.*

I NEED TWO DOUBLE A BATTERIES!

WH-WHAT CAN I POSSIBLY DO?!

WHAT ?!

MAKE SURE THEY'RE ALKA-LINE!

OKAY! I'LL BUY THEM RIGHT NOW!

24

CLNK CLNK

THANKS!

You're a real life-saver!

I DIDN'T KNOW... YOU RAN ON... BATTERIES.

Huff!

Huff!

NO!

WANNA PLAY?

BOOP BEEP

THAT WAS ALL FOR A VIDEO GAME?!

NOW WHERE WAS MY LAST SAVE POINT?

THIS SHOULD GET IT WORKING.

BEEP BOOP

CLK

RIGHT! LET ME HANDLE THIS!

UH... MY BIKE CHAIN FELL OFF.

...

REALLY? YOU NEED MY HELP?

I NEED YOUR HELP!

WAIT! DON'T LEAVE!

WHAT'RE YOU SO MAD ABOUT?

BEEP

BEEP

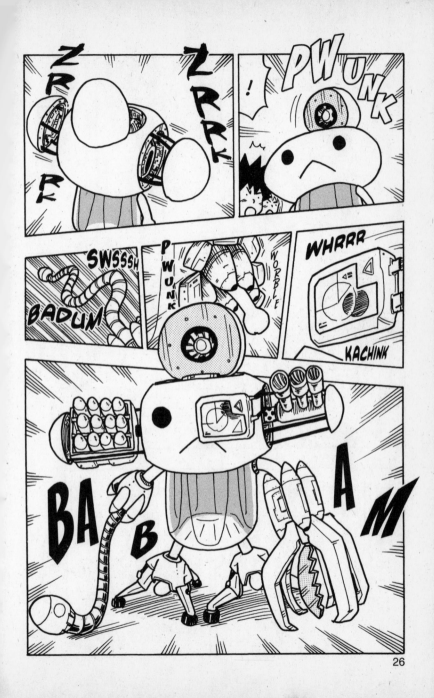

CHAPTER 4
PET Goes Round and Round

31

THWOOSH THWOOSH

LEGS.

CHING CHING

ARMS ...

I'M PET! A SUPER ROBOT SENT FROM THE RECYCLING PLANT TO REPAY NOBORU FOR RECYCLING ME!

DA- MUUU

READY FOR ACTION!

HUH?

I'VE GOT IT! THIS IS HOW I'LL REPAY YOU TODAY!

BA- BMP

TURN

LET ME TAKE A LOOK AT THIS.

PA-PA-PA! DON DON!

And gimme my juice back.

DUDE, YOU NEED A NEW INTRO.

34

WHA-WHAT'S GOING ON IN THERE?!

PET IS DEFEATED.

FTT FTT

PET MAKES AN OFFER THE MONSTER CAN'T REFUSE.

HERE WE GO!

SHAAA! SK

AT LONG LAST...

THE SUPER-STRONG MONSTER BEAST APPEARS!

HOW'D YOU DO IT?

WHAT? YOU BEAT THE GAME?

I'D RATHER NOT SAY.

WHAT?! THAT'S NOT HOW I WANTED TO WIN!

..PAN-PA-PAAN!

ONCE AGAIN PET SAVES THE DAY.

DEFEATED

THE MONSTER IS DEFEATED.

CHAPTER 5
Multilingual PET

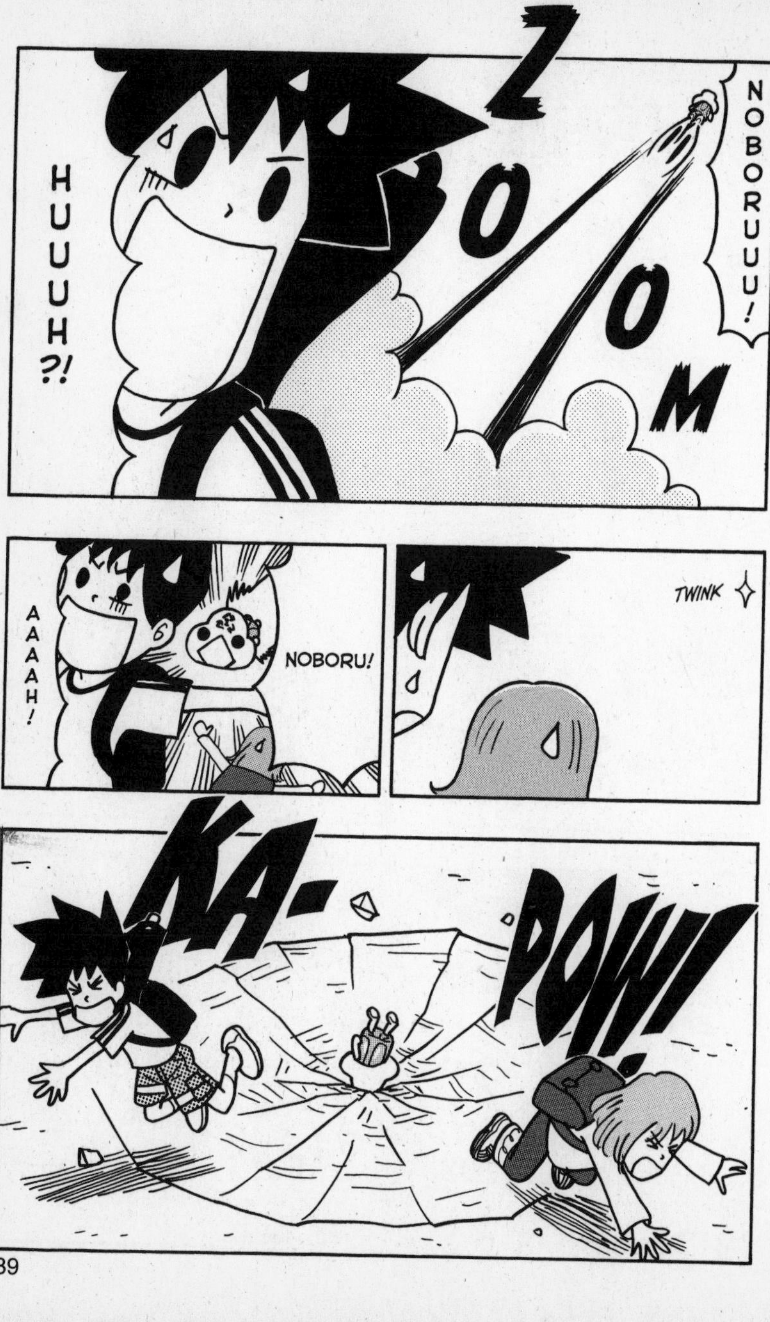
NOBORUUU!
ZOOM
HUUUUH?!
TWINK
NOBORU!
AAAAAH!
KA-POW!

40

IF I CAN'T DO IT, I CAN'T DO IT.

FOR SHOW?! WHAT KIND OF ROBOT ARE YOU?!

IT WAS JUST FOR SHOW.

BUT YOU NODDED AT HIM!

DO SOMETHING! I NEED SOME HELP!

And why do I have to carry you?

RUSTLE RUSTLE

HEY! YOU CAN'T GO BACK IN THERE!

R-REALLY?

THAT CHANGES EVERY-THING!

TMP

WHY DIDN'T YOU SAY SO?

YOU'RE IN TROUBLE?

SINCE WHEN HAVE YOU HAD THAT?!

ACTIVATING FIVE LANGUAGES FUNCTION!

...ALLOWS ME TO TRANSLATE FIVE DIFFERENT LANGUAGES!

MY FIVE LANGUAGES FUNCTION...

USE THE SWITCH ON THE BACK OF MY HEAD TO CHOOSE THE LANGUAGE YOU WANT.

OKAY.

HERE'S HOW IT WORKS:

THAT'S PRETTY IMPRESSIVE.

AWESOME!

Hello!

Blah blah blah!

THEN, PLACE ME BETWEEN YOURSELF AND THE PERSON YOU'RE SPEAKING WITH. ACTIVATE THE LANGUAGE FUNCTION AND YOU CAN TALK AS FREELY AS YOU WANT.

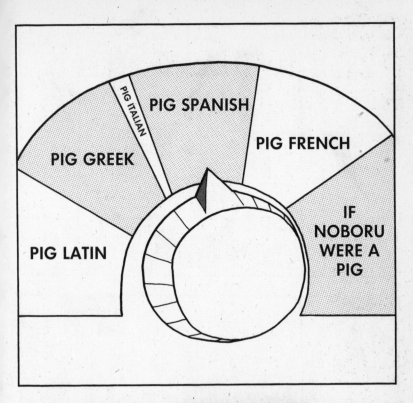

44

CHAPTER 6
PET, the One-Bottle Rescue Team

46

47

48

49

50

51

52

CHAPTER 7

PET to the Rescue!

57

58

TOOLS
- PLASTIC BOTTLE
- BOX CUTTER
- TAPE

FINISHED

■ USE A BOX CUTTER TO CUT THIS PART OUT.

※ ASK A GROWN-UP TO HELP YOU!

● COVER THE OPENING WITH TAPE!

PET

BOAT

VERSION

CAREFUL NOW...

SPLISH

WHAT IS THIS? ARTS AND CRAFTS?!

TA-DA

PET!

AAAAH!

CHAPTER 8
PET Goes to the Dogs

MY DADDY BOUGHT HIM FOR ME. ISN'T HE CUTE?

WHERE'D YOU GET THAT DOG?

PUBLIC PARK

WOOF! WOOF!

WOOF! WOOF!

I WISH I HAD A DOG, TOO.

LUCKY!

NOBORU YAMADA, AGE 9.

HEY, IT'S PET!

NOBORU!

MY FAMILY WOULD NEVER GET ONE!

NO WAY, NO HOW!

JUST ASK YOUR PARENTS FOR ONE.

63

Whine...

I'M NOT GONNA TAKE HIM FROM YOU!

HUH?

TAP TAP

HEY, NOBORU.

THEY'RE NOTHING SPECIAL.

PFFT! WHAT'S SO GREAT ABOUT DOGS ANYWAY?

REALLY? CAN I?

HERE!

Pillbug

HEY! THIS ISN'T EVEN A DOG!

BOTTLE DOGGIE?

Come here, boy?

TWEET

BOTTLE DOGGIE! COME HERE, BOY!

OF COURSE!

DOES IT HAVE TO BE A DOG?

67

SNIFF

WIGGLE

PAD PAD

WAG' WAG

TA-DA

ACK! BRING BACK BOTTLE DOGGIE! BOTTLE DOGGIE!

DOWN BOY!

Woof! Woof!

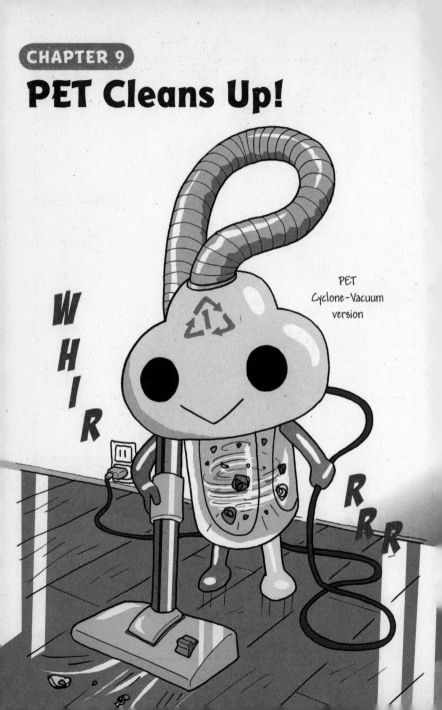

CHAPTER 9

PET Cleans Up!

PET
Cyclone-Vacuum
version

WHIR

RRR

70

71

FLIP FLIP

THIS ISN'T ABOUT PAYING ME BACK THIS TIME!

WAIT A SECOND!

...READY TO ROLL!

PET...

THERE'S A DIFFERENCE, SEE?

YOU MADE THIS MESS, SO YOU HAVE TO CLEAN IT UP!

WHAAAT?!

THEN I'M NOT DOIN' IT.

74

BA-BAM!

OPERATION PET CLEANUP!

I'LL DEFINITELY GET TO THE PARK IN TIME!

GREAT!

I CAN GET THIS MESS CLEANED UP WITHIN FIVE MINUTES!

WOW! COOL!

CALCULATING AMOUNT OF CLEANING.

BEEBEEBEEBEEP

SWING

PLOP PLOP

SWEEP

SWEEP

MANGA

BWOOO

THEN THEY ARE DRIED...

UNTIL ALL PIECES ARE MICROSCOPIC.

CHOP

CHOP

FIRST, THE GARBAGE DUMPED INTO PET'S HEAD IS CHOPPED UP INTO TINY PIECES.

ALL DONE!

PAH-TOOEY.

WHA... ?!

My manga! ...

...AND HARDENED INTO TINY PELLETS.

Meet Plaz!

Plastic Bottles

Ah, this feels like home.

Go back.

79

84

Meet Alu!

89

90

PET's Piggy Bank

SINCE WHEN DID YOU START CHARGING?!

PET'S REPAYMENT SAVINGS

PLEASE REPAY ME FOR MY GOOD DEEDS.

THAT'S ALL I HAVE!

Cheapskate!

Quit complaining!

ONLY A DIME?!

CHING

IT'S NO USE.

NNNGH!

HNNNGH!

HRRRR!

YOU LITTLE...

Here we go!

FINE! NOW TO PERFORM A GOOD DEED WORTH 10 CENTS!

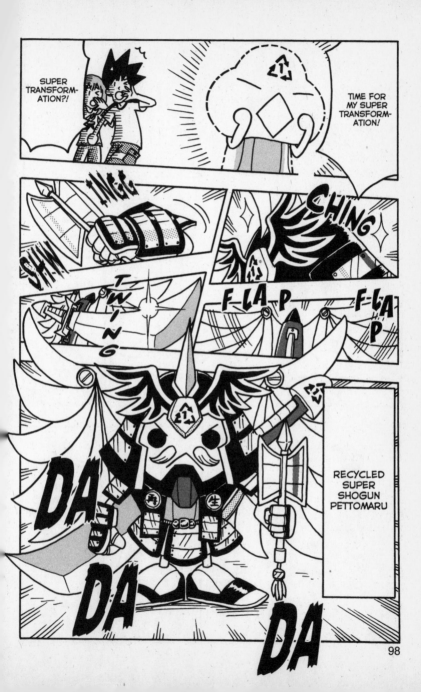

98

LOOK! IT'S PLAZ!

TINK
TINK
TINK
TINK

T W I S T

FFT

...IS PET'S ASSISTANT, MADE FROM RECYCLED PLASTIC!

SLOOP

PLAZ...

HOW DARE YOU MAKE ME LOOK BAD!

Nnngh!

THANKS, PLAZ...

HE DID IT!

UH-GA-GA-GA...

100

CHAPTER 13
Meet P-2!

HMM...

NOBORU YAMADA, AGE 9.

NO OPENING!
MANAGER

BATTLE CARD
BATTLE CARD
BATTLE CARD
BATTLE CARD

HMM, AND I CAN'T TELL WHAT'S INSIDE.

DON'T ASK ME!

BATTLE CARD
BATTLE CARD
BATTLE CARD
BATTLE CARD

WHICH PACK SHOULD I GET?

SWSH

103

DON'T TELL ME. YOU'RE TRYING TO GUESS WHAT'S INSIDE.

RUSTLE RUSTLE

MAYBE IT'S THIS ONE.

RUSTLE

RUSTLE

SPACE HERO

SO? YOU WANTED SOMETHING?

SPACE HERO FIGURINE

ALRIGHT! I'LL GO WITH THIS ONE!

WHOA!

W R R P

OKAY!

YES, BUT YOU CAN'T OPEN UP THE BAGS.

I SEE! YOU WANT ME TO FIND A CERTAIN CARD!

BATTLE CARD

105

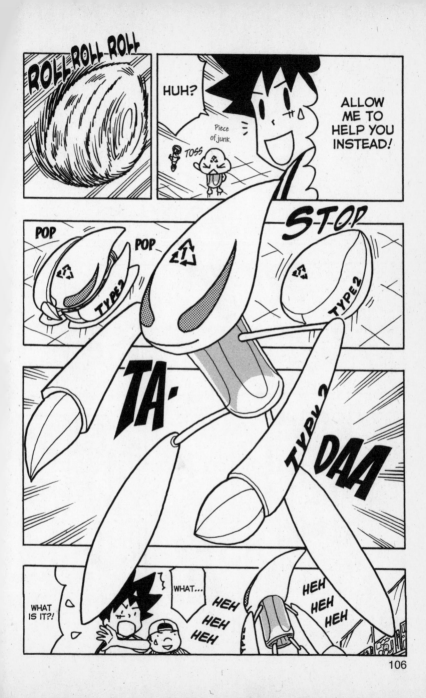

106

P-2?

IT'S P-2!

P-2

ITS MOST UNIQUE FEATURE IS ITS LARGE BUT SUPER LIGHTWEIGHT BODY.

IT'S A NEW MODEL OF GOOD-DEED ROBOT, BORN FROM ANOTHER PLASTIC BOTTLE THAT NOBORU RECYCLED.

P-2 (PROPER NAME: PET 2.0)

TYPE 2

AWESOME!

SHINY

THAT'S AS MUCH AS ABOUT 20 PENNIES!

TWINKLE

ITS TOTAL WEIGHT IS A SCANT 50 GRAMS!

108

CHAPTER 14
PET vs. P-2

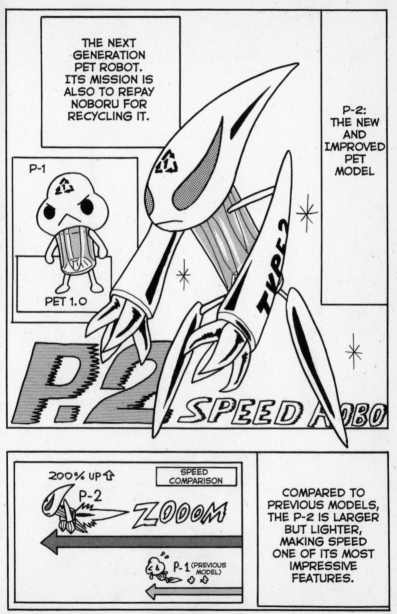

THE NEXT GENERATION PET ROBOT. ITS MISSION IS ALSO TO REPAY NOBORU FOR RECYCLING IT.

P-1

PET 1.0

P-2: THE NEW AND IMPROVED PET MODEL

P.2 SPEED ROBO

SPEED COMPARISON

200% UP ⇧

P-2

ZOOOM

P-1 (PREVIOUS MODEL)

COMPARED TO PREVIOUS MODELS, THE P-2 IS LARGER BUT LIGHTER, MAKING SPEED ONE OF ITS MOST IMPRESSIVE FEATURES.

WHAT'S THE PROBLEM?!

TELL ME ABOUT IT!

I know, I know.

I HAVE NO IDEA WHAT HE'S SAYING.

INSIDE ONE OF THESE PACKS...

BATTLE CARD

READY?

Sheesh!

I'LL EXPLAIN AGAIN. SLOWLY.

LEVEL 10

BLACK KNIGHT

THIS IS THE RAREST CARD OF ALL.

BLACK KNIGHT

PART 7

I WANT YOU TO FIND IT WITHOUT OPENING THE PACKS!

...IS THIS RARE BLACK KNIGHT CARD.

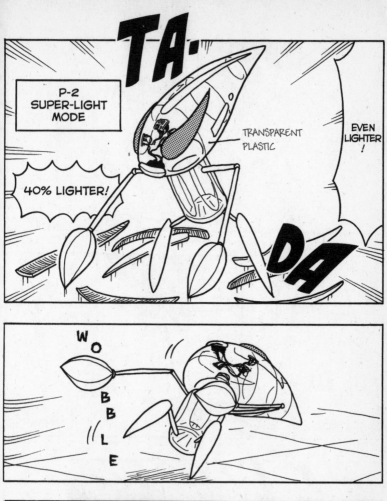

115

CHAPTER 15

It's Alive!

118

121

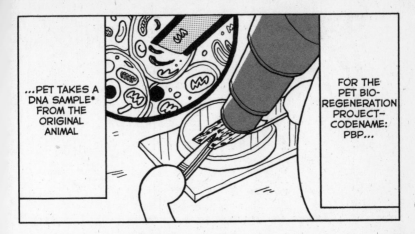

...PET TAKES A DNA SAMPLE* FROM THE ORIGINAL ANIMAL

FOR THE PET BIO-REGENERATION PROJECT— CODENAME: PBP...

...TO CREATE AN EXACT COPY.

...AND USES IT ...

YOU'VE NEVER DONE THIS BEFORE?!

THE PBP DREAM LAUNCH

IT BEGINS TODAY!

HERE GOES NOTHING!

ALL RIGHT!

Go, big brother!

Hooray! Hooray!

*DNA HOLDS ALL OF THE INFORMATION THAT MAKES EACH LIVING THING UNIQUE!

123

CHAPTER 16
PET, the Recycling Ninja

127

130

132

...4
...5
...

1...
2...3

PUBLIC PARK

WE'RE STILL ONE PLAYER SHORT FOR THE GAME.

NOBORU YAMADA, AGE 9.

ONLY FIVE PLAYERS, HUH?

GUESS I'LL HAVE TO ASK PET.

SHAKE SHAKE SHAKE

ANYONE ELSE WE COULD INVITE?

CHAPTER 17
This Is PET's Home Base

FOOMP

WHRRR

AT THE RECYCLING PLANT...

CHUNG

CHUNG

SWISH

SWISH

SWISH

CLUNK

CLUNK

CLUNK

CLUNK

EVERY DAY, THOUSANDS OF RECYCLED ROBOTS ARE MADE.

...FOR THEIR MASTERS TO CALL!

WHEN THEY'RE NOT IN USE THEY JUST WAIT...

Noboru Yamada ONLY

WHIRRR

Bob Smith

THEY ARE ALL SENT TO THE PEOPLE WHO RECYCLED THEM.

Noboru Yamada

WHIRRR

137

138

140

CHAPTER 18
PET's Secret Gadgets

DOB
DOB
DOB

MEANWHILE, BACK AT HOME BASE...

DOB

C'mon! I wanna play with Bottle Doggie, too!

DRAG DRAG DRAG

DOB

DOB

CLK CLK CLK CLK

THEY'RE CALLING YOU AGAIN!

PET! WE NEED YOUR HELP!

AW, MAN.

YOU ALWAYS SAY THAT!

NO FAIR!

AS SOON AS I'M DONE!

143

144

WHENEVER NOBORU IS IN TROUBLE, PET CAN CHOOSE FROM 108 SECRET GADGETS...

DOOM

...HELP NOROBU!

Hmmm...

Now let's see...

...SPECIFICALLY DESIGNED TO HELP PET...

WEIRD. LEMME SEE!

LOOK WHAT I FOUND!

CHECK THIS OUT!

RUMMAGE
RUMMAGE
RUMMAGE

AHA!

146

WHAAAT?!

WHAT'RE WE
SUPPOSED
TO DO WITH
THIS?!

COME
BACK
HERE!

ZOOM

CHAPTER 19
A PET for Every Occasion

152

POP!

LEAVE IT TO ME!

ALRIGHT!

DID SOMEONE SAY "TROUBLE"?!

LISTEN, WE'RE IN REAL TROUBLE HERE. MOM BACKED INTO A DITCH!

SHWRRRRL

PET HOOK AND WIRE!

Ooooh!

Wow!

THIS WIRE'S SO TOUGH, NOTHING CAN BREAK IT!

GRRT

KACHING

GRRT

SECRET GADGET #28—PET HOOK AND WIRE.

154

155

156

CHAPTER 20

Meet Tiny Tin!

But First:

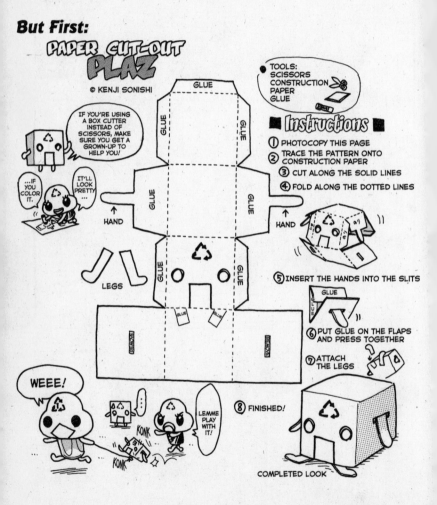

PAPER CUT-OUT PLAZ

© KENJI SONISHI

IF YOU'RE USING A BOX CUTTER INSTEAD OF SCISSORS, MAKE SURE YOU GET A GROWN-UP TO HELP YOU!

...IF YOU COLOR IT.

IT'LL LOOK PRETTY...

TOOLS:
SCISSORS
CONSTRUCTION PAPER
GLUE

Instructions

① PHOTOCOPY THIS PAGE
② TRACE THE PATTERN ONTO CONSTRUCTION PAPER
③ CUT ALONG THE SOLID LINES
④ FOLD ALONG THE DOTTED LINES
⑤ INSERT THE HANDS INTO THE SLITS
⑥ PUT GLUE ON THE FLAPS AND PRESS TOGETHER
⑦ ATTACH THE LEGS
⑧ FINISHED!

GLUE

HAND

HAND

LEGS

WEEE!

KONK

KONK

LEMME PLAY WITH IT!

COMPLETED LOOK

158

*TIN CANS ARE MADE MOSTLY FROM STEEL.

160

GYARE

UM, I'M REALLY IN A HURRY, SO I'LL JUST CLOSE IT MYSELF.

Heh heh heh.

CLIP

GOOONG

What power.

HUUUH?!

CLANG

PYOP

STEEL LOCK!

TUG TUG

IF YOU INSIST!

OKAY! FINE! PLEASE DO IT, TINY TIN!

HUH?

DANGLE

Wacha...

PLEASE, ALLOW ME TO CLOSE THE DOOR.

Charge It Up, PET!

RECYCLED GOOD-DEED ROBOT PET

WHAT? YOU WANT ME TO RECHARGE YOUR CELL PHONE?

THANK GOOD-NESS!

Phew!

I CAN HANDLE THIS, NO PROBLEM!

THADUMP THADUMP

Uh-huh. I see...

LET ME TAKE A LOOK AT THIS GIZMO.

CELL PHONE CHARGER VERSION!

RRRRUMBL

TRANS-FORM!

168

169

NOW LISTEN CLOSELY, NOBORU. THE MAIN BATTERY CAN BE FOUND DEEP INSIDE MY HEAD.

IT'S A LARGE, WHITE OBJECT.

BATTERY

1200V

I SEE IT.

Good luck, Noboru.

BATTERY

PET TYPE I

1200V

⚠ 1200V

THERE SHOULD BE SIX WIRES COMING FROM IT. THREE ON THE RIGHT AND THREE ON THE LEFT.

THE THICKEST WIRE ON THE LEFT SIDE.

WHICH IS IT?

1... 2... 3...

CLICK

ALL RIGHT! CONNECTING... NOW!

I FOUND IT!

172

CHAPTER 22

Meet the Can Crew!

174

177

179

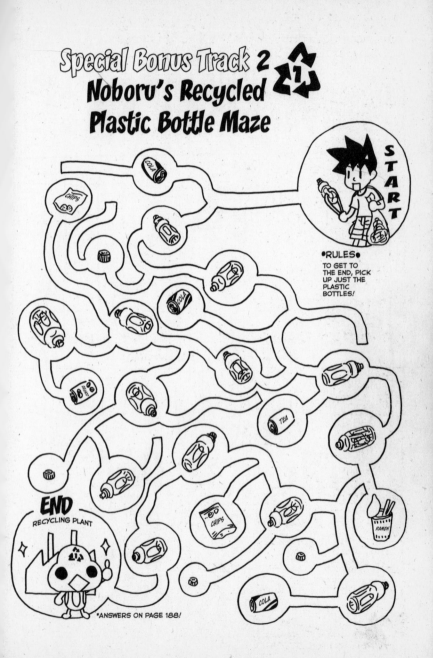

Special Bonus Track 2
Noboru's Recycled
Plastic Bottle Maze

START

•RULES•

TO GET TO
THE END, PICK
UP JUST THE
PLASTIC
BOTTLES!

END

RECYCLING PLANT

*ANSWERS ON PAGE 188!

Special Bonus Track 3

FIND THE FIVE DIFFERENCES BETWEEN THE TOP AND BOTTOM PICTURES!

*ANSWERS ON PAGE 188!

Special Bonus Track 5

HOW TO DRAW PET

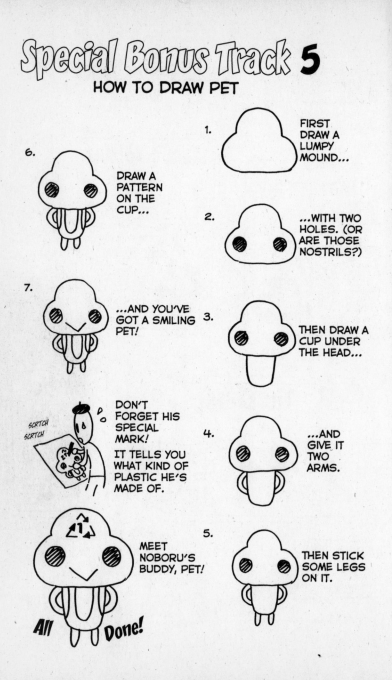

1. FIRST DRAW A LUMPY MOUND...

2. ...WITH TWO HOLES. (OR ARE THOSE NOSTRILS?)

3. THEN DRAW A CUP UNDER THE HEAD...

4. ...AND GIVE IT TWO ARMS.

5. THEN STICK SOME LEGS ON IT.

6. DRAW A PATTERN ON THE CUP...

7. ...AND YOU'VE GOT A SMILING PET!

SCRTCH SCRTCH

DON'T FORGET HIS SPECIAL MARK! IT TELLS YOU WHAT KIND OF PLASTIC HE'S MADE OF.

MEET NOBORU'S BUDDY, PET!

All Done!

Special Bonus Track Answers

Noboru's Recycled Plastic Bottle Maze

A Note About Recycling Symbols

In Japan, where *Leave It to PET!* originated, recycling is an important part of everyday life. While in the United States we only have one symbol ♻ that's used on most things that are recyclable, in Japan, just about every material has a symbol of its own. For example:

This is the symbol for recyclable **aluminum**.

This is the symbol for recyclable **steel**.

This is the symbol for recyclable **plastic other than PET bottles**.

The symbol for recyclable polyethylene terephthalate — the kind of plastic most plastic bottles are made of — can be found all over the world. Sometimes it appears with the word **"PETE"** instead of **"PET."**

Coming Soon!

The hijinks continue in the next volume of **Leave It to PET!**

Recycled robots are popping up in all
shapes and sizes. There's Baggs the plastic
bag, the amazing transforming Five Cups,
and the wise Papa-PET. Where are these robots
coming from, and why are they here?

All is revealed in volume 2 of *Leave It to PET!*

MORE GREAT MANGA FROM

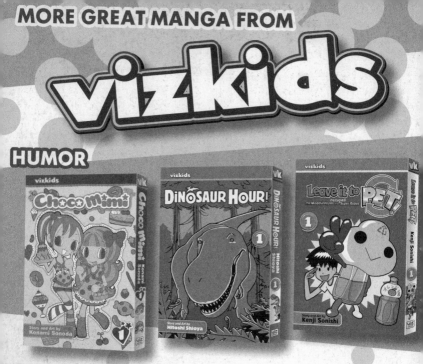

vizkids

HUMOR

ACTION / ADVENTURE

www.vizkids.com

This is the end of the book!

To properly enjoy this **VIZ Kids** comic, please turn it around and begin reading from right to left. This book has been printed in the original Japanese format in order to preserve the orientation of the original artwork. Have fun with it!